AXEL AND AVA AS CAT SITTERS

Axel and Ava as Cat Sitters

Story by ***Tuula Pere***
Illustrations by ***Nyamdorj Lkhaasuren***
Layout by ***Peter Stone***
Edited by ***Susan Korman***

ISBN 978-952-357-465-6 (Hardcover)
ISBN 978-952-357-466-3 (Softcover)
ISBN 978-952-357-467-0 (ePub)
First edition

Published 2021 by Wickwick Ltd
Helsinki, Finland

Originally published in Finland by Wickwick Ltd in 2021
Axel and Ava as Cat Sitters, ISBN 978-952-357-465-6

Axel and Ava as Cat Sitters

TUULA PERE · NYAMDORJ LKHAASUREN

WickWick
Children's Books from the Heart

Axel rings Ava's doorbell. He has news about a neighbor for his playmate.

"Becca has a new cat!" Axel explains excitedly.

"Where did she get it?" Ava asks.

"From the animal shelter for homeless cats," Axel says.

The buddies decide to go to the neighbor's right away to see the cat. Becca smiles and welcomes them. But the cat peeks timidly at the children from behind her.

“Abandoned cats are often shy,” Becca explains. “Many don’t trust people at first.”

Axel and Ava are sitting on Becca's couch. The cat watches them from a safe distance.

"It's best to let the cat get to know you slowly. It may take a while, but we're not in a hurry," says Becca.

"That's right," Axel sighs, a bit disappointed.

“Can you keep an eye on my cat for a little while?” Becca asks. “I’ll fetch some food for it from the shop.”

“We’re good cat sitters,” Ava assures her.

The children still want to play with the cat.

“Maybe we could come up with something fun together,” Ava says as Becca leaves.

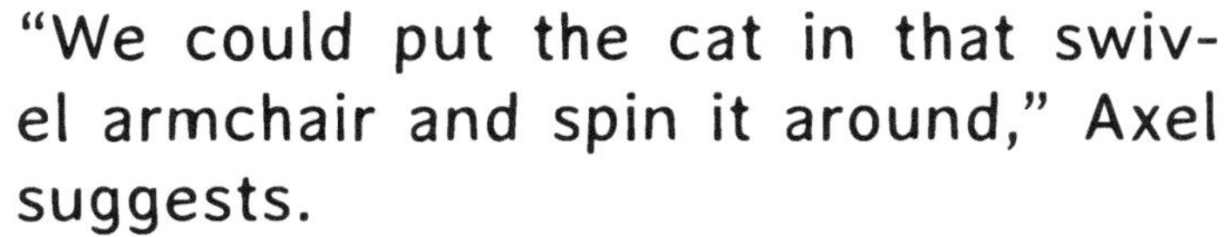

"We could put the cat in that swivel armchair and spin it around," Axel suggests.

"Yes, like a carousel!" Ava says.

However, the cat doesn't want to come into children's arms. It withdraws farther.

"I know!" Ava says. "Cats like fish. Maybe we can find a little treat in Becca's refrigerator."

The children place a small piece of smoked fish on the armchair. The delicious scent attracts the cat to come and taste.

Axel gets excited and starts to spin the chair around. “Some speed now!”

Like a flash, the cat escapes under Becca’s bed.

“We have to find something that it likes,” Ava says.

“I’ve heard that cats love to be warm,” Axel says.

The children find a wool blanket on the bed.

“When we wrap this around the cat, it will feel comfortable,” Ava suggests.

But the cat keeps hiding. Axel walks to one side of the bed, while Ava waits on the other. She is ready to wrap the cat in the wool blanket as soon as it comes out.

"Now!" Axel cries out.

Ava throws the blanket over the cat and tries to lift the pet into her arms.

The cat does not like the surprise. It hisses and wriggles under the blanket.

"I can't keep it in place. You have to help me!" Ava says.

When Axel tries to lift the captive cat, it gets angry.

“Ouch! The cat scratched my hand!” Axel shows Ava the wound.

Ava is alarmed when the cat takes off. “Where is the cat going?”

The cat rushes to the balcony.

In a second, the cat jumps over the balcony railing.

"Help, it's going to die now!" Ava screams in horror.

Axel is worried. "Becca will be so angry!"

The children peek over the edge.

Under the balcony stands Becca, who has just returned from the shop. She holds the frightened cat in her arms.

"Fortunately, I live on the second floor!" she says sternly.

Becca brings the cat in and wants to know exactly what happened. Axel and Ava speak at the same time.

"We didn't mean to hurt the cat!" the children say.

"I know that," Becca says. "But as I told you, it's best to give a rescued cat some time to get used to new people and a new home."

Becca takes care of the wound in Axel's hand and then pours some food for the cat into a bowl.

Everyone quietly watches the cat eat. Afterward, it washes its paws and face, and looks pleased.

"Can we come again tomorrow if we promise to be really calm?" the kids ask.

"Of course!" Becca says, smiling. "Soon you'll have a new friend."

The cat climbs onto the wool blanket and closes its eyes. A soft purring tells Axel and Ava that it feels safe again.

Lightning Source UK Ltd.
Milton Keynes UK
UKHW051815310822
408125UK00002B/102